A GEEKS AND THINGS COZY MYSTERY

# Have and Hold

## S.E. BIGLOW

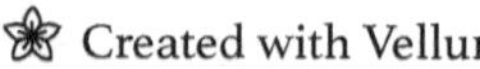 Created with Vellum

1

---

A crisp blanket of snow covered the front yard as Kalina stared out the second-story bedroom window. They didn't get a lot of snow on the coast. It usually turned to rain by the time it reached the small town of Ellesworth but today, in late January, the storm was raging and heavy. It buffeted the windows and the wind howled in the distance. Her attention diverted to the slender stick in her fingers: a positive pregnancy test. She'd had her suspicions but this confirmed it. She supposed she was lucky that she and Chris were already getting married. Still, she wanted to wait until after the wedding to share the news. She didn't want him to feel pressured into tying the knot just because of a baby. She also needed to get used to the idea of a child. She hadn't been against the idea of being a mother, but it hadn't really been in her life plan.

Still, it brought a certain sense of excitement and she knew her mother would be thrilled. She hid the test in a wad of tissues and tossed them in the trash just as the bedroom door opened and Chris appeared in his dress uniform. Since he'd made detective he hadn't needed to be in uniform. But today was a special day. After almost nine months without a captain, Chris had finally accepted the appointment.

"Well, don't you look handsome," she said and pulled him in for a kiss.

"You're going to be there right beside me," he said when she'd pulled away.

"You earned this. I'm so proud of you."

"I don't know about that. A man that I respected turned out to be a killer. I got this job because someone else murdered little old ladies."

"Chris, come on. You know you earned this. You put in a lot of hard work to keep this town and its people safe."

"I wouldn't be half as good at it without you."

"I don't know what you're talking about." She'd only been involved in a few cases but Chris had always been the one to get the credit.

"Yes, you do. I know I can't stop you from being curious."

"I'm just a lowly shop owner," she said with a sly smile.

"I just worry one day it will get too dangerous."

"I'll be fine. I promise."

He settled on the bed to lace up his shoes and Kalina took the break in conversation to put on earrings and tame her short curls into submission. She studied her reflection in the mirror, scrutinizing her waistline to see if she was showing yet. She couldn't spot any noticeable difference so her secret seemed safe.

"So have you talked to your mom about coming down for the wedding?" she asked.

"Yeah. I called her the other day. She's going to be here for everything. She said she was sending over a present early. Her instructions were very clear to open it before the wedding."

"That's kind of strange."

His reflection shrugged. "She's a little weird sometimes. But I figure I'm the last kid to get married so I'll humor her."

"I get that." She was the second of two siblings getting married in her family too.

"I have to admit I'm happy you didn't want a big ceremony," he said and moved to stand behind her, wrapping his arms around her waist.

Breath caught in her chest for a split second before she exhaled and leaned into him. "A big, flashy affair just isn't us. Besides, we're paying for everything and a cop's salary and what I make from the shop isn't the big bucks. So we do what we can."

"Exactly." He kissed her cheek and released his grip.

She checked herself in the mirror one last time before following him downstairs. She paused before going down to consider how far they'd come. They'd been engaged since Thanksgiving and had only been living together since then as well so they'd taken a few months to figure out what they wanted and who was on the guest list. She'd settled on a dress around Christmas but had to pay for it in installments. People liked their comics and other nerdy paraphernalia but the dress was still more than she felt comfortable paying for in a lump sum.

"Come on, we don't want to be late," Chris called, holding out her coat.

"Right, sorry."

She hurried down the stairs and let him help her into her coat. She wrapped a thick scarf over her face and pulled on gloves before they braved the snow. Chris opened the front door to find a package perched on the front steps, covered in a thin layer of snow. He picked it up and heard something move inside. He stepped back inside.

"We're going to be late if we open your mom's gift now," Kalina said.

"I don't know that this is from her. No return address."

It was addressed only to Detective Christian Harper. Kalina peered at the postage. "It's from the right zip code though."

"They aren't going to start without the guy

getting the promotion. We can be a couple minutes late," he said and fished in his pocket for his keys. He kept a pocket knife attached and slid the blade along the tape on the top of the box. He folded back the flaps to find a small jar with clear liquid inside. The jar held a human finger with a sparkly engagement ring. Kalina tried not to scream but the sound still came out as a strangled moan. She'd seen dead bodies before but somehow the severed finger was worse. It ignited too many questions that she didn't want to contemplate: chiefly whether the finger's owner was still alive. Chris moved with quick steps to the kitchen—ignoring the snow he tracked across the floor—and flipped on the light.

"Why would someone send you a finger?" Kalina rasped.

"I have no idea," he answered and pulled out his phone. "But I don't think this is a coincidence."

## 2

Kalina kicked off her boots and went in search of a towel to clean up the mess Chris had tracked in while he stood by the sink, phone pressed to his ear. Her own phone buzzed in her pocket, reminding her that they were already late for the ceremony. She bent down to wipe away the mess just as Chris's call connected.

"Jimmy, it's Chris. I need you to send someone over to my house immediately. You know what, why don't you just come yourself?" A pause and then, "Someone's sent me a finger in a jar."

Kalina tossed the sopping paper towel in the trash as Chris hung up and rubbed his forehead with the back of his hand. She watched him exhale a slow breath and toyed with the diamond on her left ring finger. The ring on the severed finger had to mean something. She bit her lower lip, mentally chastising herself for jumping into the investigation. Chris didn't need her help.

"What do you think?" he asked after such a long pause that she jumped.

"I think they'd better reschedule the ceremony because someone sent the acting captain of the department a human finger."

He smiled and shoved his phone in his pocket. "I meant about the finger."

"I have no idea. I didn't really take a good look. It isn't something you expect to come in the mail."

"Yeah. Jimmy and some lab techs are coming over to look at it."

"Can't we just bring it to the station since we were heading there already?"

"No. I don't want to expose it to the elements more than necessary. It's better if they examine it here."

"OK."

She steeled herself to head back into the living room. Her stomach churned at the thought of having to examine the finger before the police had their chance and she didn't think it had anything to do with the new life growing inside her. She took shallow breaths as she bent down to examine the jar that held the finger. It looked as normal as a finger cut off its hand could. Its owner was dark-skinned, Hispanic or Black perhaps. The nail was trimmed and French manicured. She wasn't a science expert but she could guess it was suspended in formaldehyde. The clear liquid distorted the cut of the ornate diamond just above the second knuckle. Still, the ring looked oddly familiar. She tried to remember where she'd seen it before but two sharp knocks at the front door broke her concentration. Before she answered the door, she snapped a quick picture of the ring on her phone, being sure to zoom in as close as possible on the ring.

"Hey, Kal," Jimmy said as she opened the door.

Jimmy was one of the youngest officers on the force but something about being in his dress blues made him look very grown up. He pulled latex gloves from his coat pocket and slipped them on, all business. A tall, female lab technician in a hat and knee-length puffy jacket ducked in behind Jimmy with a field kit. Chris emerged from the kitchen and immediately pointed to the box sitting on the living room table.

"Any idea when it arrived, Captain?" Jimmy asked, addressing Chris by the title he had not yet received.

"It had to have been in the last hour or so. I didn't see anything earlier." He turned to Kalina. "Did you see anything?"

"No. The windows upstairs usually give a good view of the front yard and the porch. I don't remember seeing anyone drop off the package.

Besides, our mail doesn't usually get delivered until the late afternoon."

The lab tech opened her kit and pulled out fingerprint powder and a brush. She leaned over and started first with the jar. "Did either of you touch this?"

"No," Kalina and Chris answered in unison.

She turned back to the purple powder and let the bristles glide over the glass jar. Nothing appeared. "Whoever sent this was careful enough not to leave prints."

She moved next to the exterior box and found a plethora of prints. Most likely the majority belonged to Chris and Kalina. His prints were already on file but hers weren't.

"Jimmy, why don't you get a fingerprint card and get Kal's prints to speed things up?"

"Sure thing, boss."

Kalina led Jimmy into the kitchen so they were out of the way and settled at the table and studied her fingernails. She'd had a manicure herself less than a week ago. The wedding was in two weeks and she'd had gel put on just to make sure they lasted long enough. Jimmy fumbled to take off the gloves and opened the ink pad.

"Just roll your finger right to left," he instructed.

Carefully, she allowed him to guide her fingers—left hand and then right—along the pad and paper until ten crisp prints lay on the page. She left him to fill out her identifying information while she scrubbed the ink from her fingers, trying not to mess up her nails. She could hear lowered whispers from the other room but her attempts to eavesdrop from beside the sink failed. For his part, Jimmy kept glancing furtively through the open doorway too.

"I don't think Chris would mind you going back in there. He called you after all. Asked for you specifically," Kalina said.

"I know. I'm just trying to figure out why someone would send him a body part. And at his house, not the station."

"Why would that matter?" She slid into the chair beside him.

"I don't know ... it just seems like if you want to taunt the police, send it to the police station. This seems like it could be personal to the captain."

"The finger has an engagement ring on it," she supplied. He would find out sooner rather than later just by looking at the jar.

Jimmy fiddled with the limp latex gloves on the table in front of him. Kalina could tell he wanted to say something but she stayed quiet until he was ready. She had an inkling of the question he wanted to ask her. But she'd let him ask the question rather than assume.

"He was almost married once," Jimmy stated.

"I know."

They'd shared all of their pasts since getting

back together. It had been an amicable break after high school, allowing them both to find themselves as adults. She got her degrees in business and he became a decorated cop. She'd dated a few guys in college and graduate school but none of them had gotten to the engagement stage. Chris, on the other hand, had gotten to the point of wedding planning but shortly before they were to walk down the aisle he'd found out that she'd been cheating on him and he'd broken things off. Kalina's mother had been upset that the ring was the same one he'd given to the cheater. She saw it as Chris holding out hope that the ring would wind up on the right person's finger. She was quite proud that the ring was now nestled between her left pinkie and middle fingers. It had quickly become a fixture on her hand so that she often forgot she was wearing it but could always tell when it was absent at night or in the shower.

"I know you tried to keep things quiet with your engagement and everything but do you think someone from his past could have found out?"

Kalina shook her head. "Even if they did, I don't see why she'd send him a severed finger. For one thing, it looks as though whoever it belongs to is Hispanic or of color and she was the one who ruined the engagement, not Chris."

"Fair enough. And I hate to ask but is there anyone who might have wanted to send something like this to you?"

"No. I had boyfriends but none that got serious enough for a proposal. I'm not sure this is personal other than to freak us out."

"All right. Well, I'm going to see what's going on out there."

"Sure."

Jimmy gathered the kit and fingerprint card and headed for the doorway leading to the living room. "You look really nice, by the way."

She smiled at him. "Thanks."

Kalina pulled her phone from her purse as soon as Jimmy was out of view and studied the photo she'd taken. There wasn't much she could do about the identity of the finger—although she secretly hoped whomever it belonged to was still alive—but she could look into the ring. It looked strangely familiar but she couldn't figure out where she'd seen it before. They'd gone ring shopping in the city, and according to Chris her engagement ring had been bought elsewhere too. But she was sure she'd seen the ring somewhere before. Its silver band, unadorned except for the large diamond, was a fairly standard design. Chewing her bottom lip, she went in search of her tablet. Chris and their guests were busy studying the jar and the package so didn't take notice as she darted upstairs in stocking feet and found what she was looking for in the study. She'd turned it into a home office. It was nice to have someone to come home to now and so she tended to do the books for the comic shop at home. The tablet sat docked to its charger on the desk and she settled in front of it.

"Where did I see this before?" she muttered to herself as she waited for the browser to load.

While she let the thought percolate, her phone issued a loud 'ding', signaling an incoming text message from her sister, Jillian. She checked it. "Mom wants to know if you wanted the emerald earrings for the wedding. Sorry for late notice."

Kalina had completely forgotten that her mother had wanted them to have matching jewelry for the wedding. It was something small she could do and it would have made their father extremely happy. The thought that her father wouldn't be walking her down the aisle brought tears to her eyes. She wiped them away and responded to the text.

"That sounds great. What jeweler is she getting them from?"

In her heart, she hoped her sister's response would give her an early clue to where the engagement ring in the jar had been purchased. If the shop was local, she could visit it on the pretense of picking out the earrings for her mother. She didn't want to drag her mother into a police investigation —about the only family she'd willingly let tag along was her nephew, AJ—but it would give her the perfect excuse if Chris asked about it.

Her sister's response took a good two minutes to come through. "Carmichael Jewelers."

"Thank you, Jill," Kalina said even though her sister couldn't hear her. She fired off a short text saying that she would check what they had and turned her attention to looking up the jeweler.

After a brief Google search, she discovered that Carmichael Jewelers was the only jewelry store in town. How she hadn't known that was a little baffling. Her embarrassment was assuaged a little when she saw that they'd only been established in town since the mid-2000s. She'd been off to college then so it made sense that she didn't know. Maybe being an unknown to the owner would be helpful in her search. Either way, she intended to pay them a visit the following morning. The snowstorm outside didn't seem to be letting up and she'd already closed down the shop for the day so the excuse of going to the shop wasn't believable.

Footsteps echoed on the stairs and she hastily shut down the search window as Chris filled the doorway to the study. He gave her an apologetic smile. "I'm so sorry about all this."

She waved his apology away. "You have nothing to be sorry for. Do they still want to do the ceremony today?"

"Yeah. We should head out in about a half hour. There isn't much we can do with the evidence until we get an ID on who the finger belongs to. Might as well carry on with our lives. It's the best way not to let the bad guys win."

She pushed herself out of the chair and wrapped him in a hug. Going out to the ceremony would give her an excuse to check out the jeweler without being too obvious.

**3**

———

The storm had let up a little by the time Kalina and Chris headed out for the rescheduled ceremony. She was working up the nerve to tell him she needed to stop by the jewelry store afterwards. She didn't want to get him involved. After all, in his dress blues, he more than screamed police. As Chris pulled into the parking lot of the station—there weren't that many people coming—he glanced over at her.

"Are you OK?"

"Huh, yeah. Just thinking. My mom wanted me to pick out some earrings for the wedding and I realized I forgot to do it."

"I could come with you if you want."

She shook her head. "No that's OK. I don't really know what I'm looking for and you have so much other stuff going on with work right now. I'll be fine."

"If you're sure."

"I am. Come on, let's get you all sworn in as captain."

They walked arm in arm through the front of the station. The small police force was assembled and in their dress uniforms as well. The mayor stood chatting with Jimmy in low tones, Kalina hoped it wasn't about the finger but they pointed in Chris's direction and her heart fell.

"I'll be right back," he said with a quick kiss to her cheek.

It turned out not to be about the finger, just logistics for the ceremony itself. She thought it was sweet that Jimmy would get to give Chris his captain's stripes. She settled in the front row and got her phone ready for some good photos. A hush fell over the bullpen and all eyes turned to the mayor, Chris and Jimmy. It was a brief exchange when all was said and done. The mayor gave a short welcome and thanked Chris for his dedicated service to keeping the town safe. Jimmy stepped up and tried to hide his excited grin as he adorned Chris's uniform. They saluted each other and then the applause from the rest of the force erupted. Kalina snapped a few quick pictures before Chris pulled her to her feet and into a bear hug.

"Thanks for being by my side for all of this," he whispered.

"There's nowhere else I'd rather be."

She could feel her phone buzzing in her purse and stepped away to see what was going on. Chris was immediately swallowed up by other people congratulating him. Her sister's number flashed across the screen.

"Hey, Jill. I'm looking into the earrings," she said automatically.

"What earrings?" AJ asked.

"Sorry, kiddo. I thought you were your mom. Grandma wants me to pick out earrings for us to wear for the wedding. Your mom reminded me this morning."

"Oh. Cool. You excited for that?"

"Of course I am." She switched the phone to her other ear. "What's up?"

"I just wanted to know how the ceremony went."

"It was fine. You could have come, Chris wouldn't have minded."

"I've kind of been on lockdown for break. Mom wants me studying for the stupid SATs."

"She's got a point. Getting good SAT scores will help you get into college."

"I know. It's just boring as hell. And I miss work."

Her nephew had been working for her during the school year on weekends and nights and she had to admit she was glad for the company. It made the small, family-owned comic shop feel homier having him around. And their shared love of all things nerdy was a bonus. Jillian had insisted he take a few months off to focus on studying for the SATs and she had agreed. She opened her mouth to tell him about the mystery package from that morning but stopped short. He would want to get involved and if someone was sending pieces of people to the police, that wasn't something she wanted her sixteen-year-old nephew caught up in.

"You still there, Aunt K.?"

"Yes, sorry. I need to go. If you want to swing by the shop tonight I can probably convince your mom you need some air and we have some inventory to sort through."

"You're the best."

Kalina laughed a little and ended the call. She felt a hand on her shoulder and spun around, coming face to face with the mayor. He was a doughy man in his forties with a thick head of blond hair and sharp, brown eyes.

"Didn't mean to scare you," he said with a smile.

"That's OK. The ceremony was really nice. Thanks for convincing him to accept the position."

"It wasn't just me. I have a feeling his beautiful fiancée had something to do with it too."

Heat warmed her cheeks and the back of her neck. "Not really. He knew he was right for the job. Would you excuse me? I have an errand I need to run for the wedding."

He nodded and she went in search of her coat at the front of the building. Jimmy lounged by the reception desk, keeping an eye on the phones.

"Hey, can you let Chris know I'm heading out?"

"Sure. Everything OK, Kal?"

"Everything's fine. I just need to run an errand. Let him know I'm taking the car."

"If you need to talk about what happened this morning, I'm here," Jimmy said in a sudden, somber tone.

"Thanks, Jimmy. I really appreciate that."

Kalina pulled on her coat and scarf and headed out to the car. She could still picture the ring in her head, sitting primly on the severed finger. Holding on to the small hope that its owner was alive—losing a single finger wasn't usually fatal—she headed to Carmichael Jewelers. It was a small shop with a clean exterior. Sets of earrings and watches adorned the front windows on display. She could see a single counter inside as she parked in one of the few spaces in the lot. Whoever owned the place had taken care to shovel the sidewalk in front of the door for ease of access. An electronic sound tolled as she pushed the door open. Gentle lighting reflected off the display cases on the center counter. It was definitely a small operation but the owner clearly had good taste in fine jewelry.

"Hello? Is anyone here?" Kalina called out.

Silence answered her at first. She took a quick

look around the small space until she spotted the single section of delicate diamond rings with a small sign announcing there was a discount for "wedding season". Finally, footsteps echoed from beyond the counter and a man in his forties appeared. He wore a sweater vest over a white dress shirt with navy blue slacks. His jet black hair lay in a natural swirl off his forehead, drawing attention away from beady grey eyes.

"Sorry, I must not have heard the bell," he said and set a ledger down on the counter.

"That's all right. I'm guessing with this storm you weren't expecting anyone to come in anyway." She unwound her scarf and undid her jacket. Her engagement ring caught the light and twinkled on her finger. His gaze zeroed in on the ring.

"How can I help you? Wedding bands perhaps?"

His directness made the little hairs on her neck stand on edge. "I'm sorry?"

He pointed to her ring. "Well, I'm assuming you're already engaged. I have some lovely bands. Is your fiancé joining us?"

"Oh, no. We have our bands picked out. We're getting married in a couple weeks and I was wondering if you had any emerald earrings I could look at for myself and my matron of honor."

"Earrings?"

"Yes. To be honest, my mother is insisting and

you know it is important to keep the mother of the bride happy."

He smiled briefly and coughed. Clearing his throat, he waved her over to a case of delicate studs. He pulled out a tray and pointed to a few of them. "How about these?"

"Um, I was thinking something that dangled. We're wearing our hair up so it would be a nice contrast."

"I'll have to see what I have in the back."

He started to move away and her gaze darted to the ledger book sitting on the other end of the counter. An idea was forming but she needed one more piece of information before she could implement it.

"Oh, actually, before you do that, there's one other thing I wanted to look at."

He gave an exasperated sigh at being interrupted but turned back to face her. "Yes?"

"A friend of mine is thinking of proposing to his girlfriend and it would be really nice if he knew what was out there. I noticed your collection. Could I take a look?"

"You're quite the busy bride, aren't you? Wedding on the horizon and checking out what's out there for other people?"

"He's still working up the nerve to buy the ring but it would go a long way if I told him there was a great jeweler with reasonable prices right here in town."

The compliment seemed to bolster the jeweler's mood and he pulled out the tray of engagement rings. She bent low to study them, looking at the tiny tags and their ID numbers. It was exactly what she'd needed. She even spotted one that looked remarkably like the one from the mystery finger. She pointed to that one and he handed it over. She committed the ID to memory before handing it back. She also noted that there appeared to be three empty spots that used to hold rings that had been sold.

"I could put it on lay away for your friend, if you'd like?"

"I'll ask him." She licked her lips and turned back toward the other display. "So, about those earrings?"

"Yes. Of course. I'll see what I can find. Just wait here a moment."

He disappeared back the way he'd come and she seized the opportunity to pour over the ledger. It was open to a page conveniently marked "Engagement Rings". Despite the three empty slots, she found only two people had come in within the last month to purchase diamonds for their sweethearts. Instead of jotting down the names and addresses, Kalina retrieved her phone from her purse and snapped a shot, making sure to zoom in close for the names of the buyers. The fact that this particular entry had been left open was a little strange but she tried to brush it off. Maybe he was just cataloging his inventory. She understood how that went.

She replaced the ledger and retreated to the other side of the counter. He returned a moment later and presented two pairs of silver earrings with simple emerald stones. They were definitely beautiful and exactly what she'd imagined wearing. She checked the price and tried not to look stunned. They were not cheap. But she only got married once and if she left without a purchase more than just her fiancé would be suspicious.

"I'll take both pairs."

"Very good. I'll just need to get your information."

"Thanks for making this so simple, Mr. Carmichael," she said.

"Oh, my name's Bruce Hempstead. Carmichael's is a franchise."

"I just assumed. I'm so sorry."

He gave her a toothy grin and boxed up the two pairs of earrings. Ten minutes later she piled back into the car and shoved the key in the ignition. She needed to share what she'd found with Chris. She was about to hit speed dial when a call came through from his number.

"Well, this is good timing. I've got something to show you," she said.

"That's good because we have an ID on the finger."

"I'll come to the station right away."

**4**

———

Kalina's heart hammered against her ribs as she made her way back across town to the station. She had a bad feeling that one of the men in the ledger was going to have a fiancée with one less finger. The parking lot was emptier as she pulled into a spot and cut the engine. The rest of the officers had returned to their patrol duties and the few townspeople who were in attendance likely had gone back to their day jobs. Kalina stowed the earrings in the glove box just to be safe before heading inside. Jimmy and Chris stood side by side at Chris's desk.

"You said you found out who the finger belongs to?" she said without waiting for them to look up from the file between them.

"Her name is Gabriella Baez," Chris answered.

The name didn't sound familiar. He showed her

a photo from a missing person's report but Kalina still didn't recognize her. She did, however, recognize the name of the person who filed the report. She pulled up the photo of the ledger she'd taken and toyed with her phone.

"What'd you find, Kal?"

"So, um, don't get mad at me. This was in plain view the whole time. I didn't even touch the pages. But it looks like a couple of guys bought engagement rings similar to the one we found from Carmichael Jewelers recently and one of them"—she zoomed into the first name—"might be connected to Ms. Baez."

Chris and Jimmy both bent forward and examined the neatly handwritten ledger for a Mr. Duncan Westford. Jimmy flipped through the pages of the missing person report and let out a sound of understanding.

"I think you're right. Mr. Duncan filed the report. Ms. Baez is his fiancée and she didn't return home after their engagement party."

"When was that?" Kalina returned the photo to its original size while Jimmy skimmed the report.

"Looks like at least three days ago."

"I doubt she cut off her own finger. If she didn't want to marry the guy she would have just returned the ring," Chris remarked and rubbed at his chin.

"But why would he report her missing if he hurt her?" Jimmy asked.

Kalina and Chris both started to speak but stopped. As they both knew, many things—money, or the promise of it, included—could be powerful motivators to falsely report a person as missing. After all, Jillian's college best friend had attempted to do just that when she knew her husband was dead and she'd had a hand in it.

"We need to contact Mr. Westford, have him confirm the ring belonged to his fiancée," Chris said.

"You aren't going to show him the finger are you?"

"No, we've had one of the lab techs remove and photograph it separately. We got lucky that her prints were in the system."

"How? She doesn't look familiar."

"She's a teacher in the state. They have to get fingerprinted before they start teaching and we have access to the database."

"Oh. So when is he coming in?"

"Not until tomorrow morning most likely. We have officers making the notification right now."

"So what do you do now?"

Chris let out a sigh. "Now I got home and celebrate my promotion with my beautiful fiancée."

Kalina smiled. "Oh, I don't know if it helps or matters but you should probably take down the name of the other person who bought a ring like Gabriella's. If it isn't her fiancé, there might be someone else out there who is at risk."

Jimmy took her phone to copy down the information before he gathered up the missing person report and his notes and headed for the reception desk. Chris tugged on his coat and hat and offered her his arm.

"Shall we?"

"Actually, I promised AJ I'd let him come by the shop and help me do some inventory."

"I thought he was taking some time off."

"He is, but he's going a little stir crazy doing constant SAT prep. Jill's going a bit overboard."

"Well, I would like to spend some time with you later."

"I won't work too late. I promise."

## 5

After stopping to grab a sandwich and bottled water, Kalina settled in the game room with the inventory boxes spread around her. She heard the back door swing open and she looked up only briefly to see her nephew kick snow off his shoes and unwind the scarf around his face.

"Thanks for doing this, Aunt K.," he said and settled into a chair beside her.

"Hey, I can use the help." *Especially when the baby comes.* She caught herself before she could voice that particular concern. Not before she'd shared the news with Chris.

"So anything new and exciting going on?" AJ probed.

"What makes you think there's anything exciting going on?"

"You sort of have that look."

Her brow furrowed. "What look?"

"The 'there's a case I'm not supposed to be looking into but I'm doing it anyway' look."

"I don't have … fine. But if you breathe a word of this to your mother, you're fired."

He mimed locking his lips and throwing away the key. "I promise."

"We got a severed finger in the mail."

"We?"

"It was sent to the house. It belongs to a woman who was reported missing a few days ago. Chris is looking into it."

"Why would someone send you a finger?"

"I have no idea. And it was addressed to Chris. I'm guessing because he's the new police captain." She raked her fingers through her hair. "But it had an engagement ring and the person who reported her missing had just bought one. Chris is supposed to talk to him tomorrow."

"Did they find her?"

"Not yet." She wanted to tell him that the woman was fine but she couldn't force the lie past her lips. "But that was my day."

"Do you think the guy hurt her … the one who bought her the ring?"

"I'd like to think not. If he cared enough to ask her to marry him, I can't imagine he'd want to cut off her finger after she'd accepted his proposal."

"You know, I don't remember anything this weird

happening before you moved back to town," AJ said with a half-smile.

"Are you saying I've bad mojo or something?"

He shrugged a shoulder. "Maybe. All I know is in the last year we've had more crazy stuff happen in town than ever before."

"Great, my nephew thinks I'm cursed and to blame for people getting killed in town."

"Not what I'm saying at all! If you weren't around to help out, they wouldn't figure out what was really going on most of the time."

"Give Chris and the rest of the force some credit. They get there eventually. And I think at this point they've kind of accepted I can be useful."

"Well they'd be dumb not to."

"I just worry that, if it isn't the fiancé, there are other people out there who could be in danger."

"Why?"

"Just a feeling." She couldn't tell him any more about the case or her hunch. Especially since she hadn't shared her worry with Chris yet and if she was going to tell anyone, it should be him.

They fell into silence as they turned their attention to the task at hand. Together, they managed to get the inventory entered into the system and organized for the usual customers to pick up their new issues. Kalina's phone gave a loud double beep at 6:30. She glanced at the screen to see a text from Chris. "See you at home."

"Hey, Aunt K. I should probably get home. Thanks for the break in monotony."

"That's a good SAT word," she teased and ruffled his hair.

He gave her an annoyed look but said nothing as he pulled on his scarf and jacket. She checked the front door to ensure it was locked before she followed him out to the small back lot. He started to trudge through the snow.

"I'll give you a ride," she called.

Her nephew's face lit up at the offer and he scrambled into the passenger seat as Kalina climbed behind the wheel and started the car.

"I hope you find the lady with the missing finger and that she's okay," he said ten minutes later, after navigating the snow piles in the center of town.

"Me too."

As soon as AJ was out of the car, she did a U-turn and headed home. She found Chris waiting for her with a glass of wine and a roasted chicken cooling on the sideboard. She hesitated as she took the glass, tipping it to her lips but not drinking any.

His gaze narrowed. "What's wrong?"

Kalina set the glass down and shook her head. "Nothing."

"Come on, after the day we had, you have to want a drink."

"I'm just not in the mood for it, I guess. Thinking about what happened makes me kind of queasy."

"Oh. Can I get you something else?"

"I'm fine."

The scent of the cooling chicken simultaneously made her mouth water and her stomach churn. She wasn't going to be able to hide things for much longer. Maybe now was the best time to spill the beans. They were only two weeks away from the wedding anyway. There was little chance he'd abruptly change his mind about marrying her.

"Actually, I need to tell you something," she said and motioned for him to sit down.

"OK. What is it?" In one fluid motion he pulled out the chair and slid onto the seat.

She settled into the seat across from him and smoothed out the winkles in the hem of her dress. She opened her mouth to speak—hoping just blurting it out would quash the fear bubbling up in her chest—when Chris's phone rang.

"It's the station. Just give me one second." He answered the call and swiveled to face the sink. "Captain Harper."

She couldn't see his facial expression and the call was turned down low enough she couldn't overhear who was on the other end of the line. Chris let out a sigh. "You're absolutely sure?" A pause. ""And there was a finger missing? The same one?"

Chris turned back to face Kalina and she knew she wasn't going to be able to share her news with him. His cheeks were suddenly drawn. "They found a body out on the beach by the water."

"Oh God. Is it Gabriella Baez?"

"No. It's a different woman. This one's white. She had ID on her. Her name is Margaret Fink. She was twenty-six."

"You think she had her finger cut off with an engagement ring on it?"

"It would be my guess." He pinched the bridge of his nose. "If Gabriella isn't dead yet, I suspect she will be soon. We might have a serial killer on our hands."

"You'll figure this out," Kalina said and twisted the still-full glass of wine in front of her by the stem. "Who do you think killed this other woman?"

"I don't know. We are still bringing Gabriella's fiancé in for questioning in the morning. All the officers told him is that we had some information on his fiancée's whereabouts and we needed to talk to him. And we'll have to look into Margaret's life to see if she also had a fiancé."

"Do you think either of the fiancés could have killed them?"

"I don't know. Honestly, if he'd just proposed to her and she'd said yes, it doesn't make sense. But then again, people have plenty of reasons to end engagements."

*Like cheating partners.*

He scrubbed at his face with the heels of his hands. "This is not how I hoped this would go."

She reached across the table to give his hand an affectionate and supportive squeeze. "I know. But you'll find out what happened."

"Sorry, what did you need to tell me?"

"Don't worry about it. It can wait. The case is more important. I understand if you want to go back to the station to wait for the field reports."

"No, I think right now I'm right where I need to be." He kissed the top of her hand. "With you."

**6**

---

Kalina barely slept that night. Her mind refused to quiet, instead spinning wild theories about some maniac chopping off unsuspecting women's ring fingers. She had held off telling Chris about the pregnancy too. He needed to be laser focused on the case. News of the baby would only distract him. When the clock read 6:07 a.m., she snuck out of bed and headed down to the kitchen to make some tea. The sun was barely above the horizon as she stared out the window above the sink waiting for the water to boil. As she stood there in the silence of the early morning, the tiny hairs on the back of her neck twitched, signaling danger.

"You're just imagining it," she mumbled to herself but it didn't stop her from checking the front step. No soggy box with a human finger waited for them this morning.

A tiny sigh of relief escaped her lips as the tea kettle whistled loudly. Several minutes later she sat on the couch in the living room, tea mug in one hand and her laptop propped on her knees. Chris had been using it the night before when she'd gone to bed. His work email sat open on the screen with a new message and attachment from Jimmy. The field report from Margaret's crime scene. Without hesitating, she opened the email and read the report.

**"The victim was found near the low tide marker on the beach. She was buried under snow and appears to have suffered blunt force trauma to the head. The left ring finger was likely severed prior to death based on clotting. Coroner estimates the victim has been dead for at least seventy-two hours; however, recent weather conditions may make proper determination difficult. A more accurate time of death will follow with the autopsy."**

Kalina scrolled down and stopped at the photos. The winter storm had preserved Margaret's face in a mask of terror. She'd seen an elderly woman look that way when she and Chris had solved the revenge killings perpetrated by the police department's former captain. It was not a sight she'd ever wanted to see again. The tea that had warmed her now roiled in her gut and she hastily set both computer and mug down to race to the downstairs bathroom. She would have liked to blame it on the morning sickness but she was nearly through the first trimester.

"Kal, are you OK?" Chris's voice came through the closed door of the bathroom a few minutes later.

She rinsed out her mouth and opened the door. "Fine."

"You're pale"—he pressed his hand to her forehead—"and clammy. I think you might be coming down with something."

"I'm not. I swear."

His gazed narrowed and he crossed his arms over his chest. "Something is going on with you. And I think it has something to do with what you wanted to tell me last night."

"I told you, it can wait. You need to focus on this case and find whoever's doing this before anyone else gets hurt."

"Right now, I need my fiancée to tell me the truth."

She relented and pushed past him out of the bathroom. "I was going to wait to tell you until after the wedding. I didn't want it to affect why we are getting married. But I'm pregnant. Almost twelve weeks."

She'd pictured his reaction in her head a million times. Stunned, slack-jawed silence. Maybe some sputtering as he tried to find words. Instead, he beamed from ear to ear and pulled her into a gentle hug. "We're having a baby!"

"Yeah. We are." She returned the hug and let all the stress of not telling him melt away.

"That explains the wine last night," he said in her ear.

"I honestly wasn't expecting this reaction," she said and leaned back to study his expression.

"We've talked about wanting kids."

"I know. Just, after the wedding."

"Technically it will be after the wedding," he said with a smirk.

She laughed a hearty belly laugh. This was why she loved him and why she wanted to spend the rest of her life with him. They stood there, wrapped in each other's arms, until Chris's phone once again interrupted their domestic bliss. Chris let out a groan and fished it out of his back pocket.

"I'll call Jimmy back later."

"No. Take it. It's probably about the case. He sent you the report this morning," she said. There was a time when she would have tried to hide her snooping but he was resigned to it these days.

"Did he?"

"It's open on the laptop. You might not want to eat anything before you look at it though."

Chris's phone stopped ringing and he hit redial while Kalina retrieved her mug of tea and went in search of breakfast. She also set the coffee percolating, knowing Chris would need at least one cup before he left for the day.

"Sorry I missed you before. What's... Jimmy, slow down and take a breath." He switched the phone to his other ear. "It went to who? No, I'll be there as soon as I can."

He ended the call and pulled a travel mug from the cabinet beside the stove. "I'm going to need that to go. Another finger's shown up."

"Did it go to the precinct?"

"No. It was sent to a reporter named Beth Finnegan. Whoever this guy is, he's getting bolder."

## 7

Kalina wanted to join Chris at the station to hear what the reporter had to say but she knew it would be better for the investigation if she wasn't present. There was still some digging she could do on her own. The name Margaret Fink was starting to ring a bell. So, as Chris hastily pulled on his coat and hat, she set about getting dressed so she could head to work. A plan was beginning to form in the back of her mind as she pulled in behind the shop a little before 8:30.

The interior was as she and AJ had left it the evening before: slightly messy but with a certain order to the chaos. She wasn't set to open for another half hour so she had time to search through the files for what she was looking for. Settling into one of the big chairs in the game room, she pulled up the roster of monthly orders. As she'd suspected, Margaret Fink had an outstanding order from a couple weeks earlier and she had listed Carter Whalen as an authorized person to pick up the orders. It wasn't as though comics were prescription drugs but many of her regulars took their collections seriously enough to only allow pick-up by certain people.

A quick bit of Facebook stalking revealed that Margaret and Carter had recently gotten engaged. She'd changed her profile picture to one of the two of them showing off the ring. Without being friends, Kalina couldn't enlarge the picture to get a good look at the ring but she had a hunch it resembled Gabriella's. She was about to dial Carter's phone number on the pretense of having him pick up her outstanding order when she realized she could at least confirm whether Carter had purchased the ring from Carmichael's.

"Damn." The curse escaped her lips before she could stop herself as the snapshot of the ledger confirmed that he was the other man on the list.

Overcome by sudden emotion, she had to sit in silence for a moment or two to collect herself. She wanted to believe it was the pregnancy hormones beginning to kick in but she was just lying to herself. Luring a man in to ask him questions about his dead fiancée was not what normal people did. Her hands shook as she entered his phone number and hit "Call". As it rang, Kalina tried to prepare herself to leave as benign a message as possible.

"Hello?" A man's baritone answered the call.

"Is this Carter Whalen?" Her voice hitched as she spoke his name.

"Yeah, who's this?"

"My name is Kalina Greystone. I own Geeks and Things here in town. I've been trying to get in touch with Margaret Fink about an outstanding order that she has waiting for her. She has you listed as someone who can pick it up."

"Oh. Sorry about that. Things have been kind of crazy lately. I can come by and pick them up if you want."

"That'd be great. If you stop by now you can get them before we open."

"Great. I'll be there as soon as I can."

She ended the call and wiped at the corners of her eyes. She needed to look presentable and as though she didn't know his fiancée had been found murdered on the beach. The fact that she could have been dead for a few days by now made her curious. He didn't seem concerned about her whereabouts or wellbeing.

Ten minutes later, she heard a knock on the front door. She'd already pulled Margaret's order and packaged it up. Carter looked a little dazed as she pulled open the front door and flipped the front sign to "Open". He was shorter than she'd expected from the picture on Facebook.

"I'm glad you could come by," she said and darted behind the front counter.

"Sure. So how much do I owe you?"

"Fifteen dollars."

"Maggie loves these things. I've never seen someone get so into graphic novels before."

She noted his use of the present tense. If he was lying, he was doing a very good job of it. She took his twenty dollar bill and handed a five back.

"So, do you know why she hasn't been by to pick them up? Usually diehard fans are very prompt with their pick-up."

Carter rubbed his neck and laughed. "That's probably my fault. We got engaged a couple weeks ago and we've been diving head first into planning. We don't want a long engagement."

"Oh. That's understandable. Congrats by the way."

"Thanks." He picked up the bag and tucked it carefully into his jacket. "She's visiting some friends out of town for a few days right now. Sort of her last hurrah before we really get buried in the planning."

He really didn't know his fiancée was dead. No one could be that good at lying without having no emotions and this guy clearly cared a great deal about the woman he'd asked to marry him. Before she could say anything, her phone rang. The Caller ID indicated it was from the station.

"Excuse me," she said and turned her back to answer the call. "Hello?"

"Hey, hon. I have a weird question for you," Chris said on the other end.

"OK. What is it?"

"You don't happen to know a Carter Whalen? He's Margaret's fiancé."

"Yes, I know that. I can stop by if you want."

"He's there with you, isn't he?" Chris's tone carried an edge of worry.

"Yeah. So I'll see you soon."

She ended the call before Chris could say anything else and turned to face Carter. He was pulling on his gloves. "That was my fiancé. He's the new police captain."

"Oh. Well, I guess congratulations are in order for you too."

"He's looking for you. He needs to talk to you about Margaret."

"Why?"

"Because they found her on the beach last night."

Carter's stare turned blank and his body swayed side to side as he took in the information. Kalina wanted to offer a hand to steady him but she'd just delivered the worst news a person could get. He didn't want her comfort.

"I need to see her," he said barely above a whisper.

"I'll take you to the station. And I'm very sorry for your loss."

**8**

---

Carter remained quiet during the short drive to the station. There were more cars in the lot than Kalina was expecting. A few more uniformed officers were heading into the building as she cut the engine and unbuckled her seatbelt. As soon as they pushed through the front doors she realized why the force was being called in. Not only did they have to speak with Carter and Gabriella's fiancé, but they were probably still questioning Beth about the finger she received in the mail. A female officer, who Kalina believed was named Vanessa, approached them as soon as the door swung shut.

"Mr. Whalen?" she said.

"Yes," Kalina answered for him.

"Please come with me. We have a few questions for you."

Carter nodded mutely and shuffled off after

Vanessa. Kalina stayed rooted to the spot just taking in the hustle and bustle of the bull pen. She finally spotted Jimmy among the crowd, seated beside a young blonde woman. She had a tissue pressed to her cheek and Kalina guessed she was Beth, the reporter. Trying to be inconspicuous, Kalina picked her way through the throng of officers until she was within eavesdropping distance.

"So just to make sure I have everything clear, you found the package this morning on your front steps," Jimmy said.

"Yes. I didn't think anything of it at first. My mother orders stuff all the time and just puts my name on it. I figured that's what she'd done but when I opened it..." Her cheeks paled and she visibly swallowed.

"Thank you." Jimmy looked around until he spotted Kalina. "I'll get someone to drive you home."

"No. God, I can't go back there."

"Well, wherever you want then."

Jimmy left the desk and joined Kalina where she stood. "Could you do me a huge favor and take her wherever she wants to go? We're a little swamped here."

"Is that OK with Chris?" Kalina asked.

"Yeah, I'm sure it is."

"How is everything else going?" She gestured around her. "I thought it was just some interviews. It looks like the whole force is here."

"The captain set up a command post for everyone to check in. Forensics and the lab and everything. He wants information as soon as its available. He's worried we've got a serial on our hands."

"But it's just Margaret, right?"

"Not anymore. They found Gabriella Baez this morning."

"On the beach?"

"Yeah. Not too far from where we found Margaret."

"That's awful."

Beth rose from the seat where Jimmy had left her and shoved her used tissue in her oversized purse. Kalina sighed and took out her keys.

"I'll take her." She wanted to stay to hear what the fiancés of the respective victims had to say but getting Beth out of the cops' collective hair was probably a better use of her time.

"Thank you so much."

Kalina approached the reporter and held out her hand. "I'm Kalina."

"I know who you are."

"Oh. Well, Jimmy said you needed a ride. Where can I drop you?"

Beth shouldered a laptop bag that had been hidden behind her chair and gestured to the front of the building. "Anywhere but here."

"OK."

Once they were out in the crisp winter air, Beth exhaled a long breath. "You probably have work to do."

"Town isn't very big. I'm pretty sure my customers can wait a few minutes while I drop you somewhere."

"Actually, I can't really face work just yet. Would it be too much of an inconvenience if I hide out at your shop?"

"Well..."

"I swear I'll stay out of your way."

Kalina forced a smile. "Sure."

"It's unbelievable how much more exciting things have been in town the last few months," Beth remarked as they climbed into the car and hit the road.

"What do you mean?"

"The police captain is really a murderer. And then there was the real estate scam that shut down construction on the new condo development. Now someone is sending people fingers."

"I take it you're a crime reporter."

"Not really. But I think I might want to be now, if my editor will let me."

"Well maybe not this story."

"Why not? It would make great headlines."

"But you're involved in the case now, since you were sent a finger. Chris—Captain Harper—

wouldn't appreciate you releasing details about the case."

"You're really close with him aren't you?"

Kalina flashed her engagement ring. "Marrying the man in two weeks."

"Oh. You're right. I should just stay out of it."

Kalina glanced at her passenger in the rearview mirror. She could see the same eagerness to solve the mystery in Beth that she saw in herself. It wasn't a bad quality to have, especially for a reporter. But this case was escalating quickly. As she pulled into the back lot behind Geeks and Things a knot started to tighten in her gut. The small diamond on her left ring finger suddenly felt very heavy. Someone was targeting recently engaged couples. They'd sent the fingers to the police and the press respectively for a reason.

"You can hang out back here," she told Beth and gestured to the empty game room. It usually didn't fill up until the afternoon.

"Thanks." Beth settled into one of the chairs and pulled out her laptop.

Kalina paused, about to ask a question, but stopped herself. Whatever Beth was working on wasn't her business.

9

Time passed quicker than Kalina expected that day. A steady stream of customers passed through the shop and she spotted Beth curled up in the back of the game room, unfazed by the small kids playing Zombie Dice at the table next to her. She seemed focused on what she was working on and Kalina supposed it was good for the woman to get buried in her work. A little after lunchtime Kalina's phone rang, displaying Chris's cell phone number on it.

"Hey, how are you holding up?" she asked as soon as she accepted the call.

"It's been crazy. How about you?"

"I'm fine. I'm babysitting the reporter. She didn't want to go back to work."

"It was nice of you to offer."

*Jimmy didn't give me a choice.* "I figured you were all so busy it was the least I could do. Dare I ask what happened with the other interviews?"

"I can't really talk about it right now. I was just calling to see if you wanted to get lunch."

On cue, Kalina's stomach gurgled loudly. "Sure. Just give me like twenty minutes. I've got a few people coming in to pick up orders that I promised would be here during their lunch break."

"I'll come by and pick you up." The line crackled as if he were putting his hand over the phone's speaker. "And I promise I'll share what I know."

"I love you," she said as the front door opened and couple of teenagers ambled in.

Before she could greet them or ask what she could help them with, Beth appeared, laptop bag swung over her shoulder. "Thanks again. I think I'm going to head out."

"Are you sure? I'm not sure they want you going home yet."

"I'll be fine. I'm just going to get some fresh air and clear my head."

With nothing else to say and no real authority to stop her, Kalina watched the blonde stride out of the shop. Kalina turned her attention back to the customers now leaning on the counter, studying the rows of freshly arrived comics on the wall behind her. In the end, they each walked away with a bag full of comics and significantly lighter allowances.

Chris arrived a little after 12:30 without food. Despite his attempt at looking cheerful, the lines around his eyes and the slightly pallid color of his cheeks told her otherwise. She wanted to just kiss him and make it all go away but that wasn't possible.

"Where's lunch?"

"I thought we could go home and I'd make you something from scratch."

"I want quesadillas," Kalina said and retrieved her coat from the back.

He offered her his arm and she took it. "Quesadillas it is."

Half an hour later, they sat across from each other at the table, munching on their food. Kalina absently ran her right index finger along the band of her engagement ring. The weight of it had dissipated some but it was still more noticeable than it had been.

"So, what did Carter and Gabriella's fiancés have to say?"

Chris blew out a breath and set his drink down. "They both claim they last saw their fiancées alive and they were very happy with their engagements. They both had alibis for the dates that Margaret and Gabriella went missing."

"How long had Gabriella been dead?"

"A day, maybe two. Definitely less than Margaret."

Kalina's brow furrowed. "But we got Gabriella's finger first."

Chris cleared his throat. "It looks like hers was mailed before Margaret's in an attempt to throw us off the trail."

She nodded in understanding and took a big bite of lunch. Chewing contemplatively, a thought occurred to her. "This may sound crazy and stupid but did you ask about what each of them was doing when the other one's fiancée went missing?"

He didn't respond right away. She studied his face as he chose his words. "You think they each killed the other one's fiancée in a *Strangers on a Train* type situation?"

"Like I said, it's probably stupid but it could be a thing, right?"

"No, it's possible. And I didn't think to even ask about that. They both seemed so believable in their grief."

"It's probably nothing. Just forget I even brought it up. I don't want to mess with your investigation."

"It's a good point and I'm going to check it out."

"You know, I just thought of something else that might be useful," she said after downing half her drink in one swallow.

"I'm listening."

"When I was at the jewelers I noticed that there were three rings missing from the display case. There were only two entries on the ledger of people who bought rings there. It seems kind of odd now. You might want to talk to the guy who runs the place."

"I'll look into that too." Chris cleared away his own plate and glass and glanced at her over his shoulder. "So, how are you really feeling?"

"I'm fine, I swear. I'm lucky that the morning sickness is really only in the morning."

"Have you been to the doctor?"

"Not yet. I'm going to make an appointment. I'm guessing I'm close to the end of the first trimester right now. I was going to wait until after the wedding. Besides, I want you to be there for everything that you can be."

"I'd love that."

She smiled at him and tucked a stray curl of red hair behind her ear. In that moment she wondered what their baby was going to look like. Would he or she have her hair or Chris's eyes or smile? There was so much to look forward to. With a kiss to her forehead, he picked up her lunch dishes and set about washing them. She suspected he would be helping out a lot more around the house in the coming months. His phone buzzed with a text alert. With his hands busy, Kalina grabbed it and read the message aloud. "It's from Jimmy. He says he sent you a link to the online edition of the afternoon paper. There's an article you're going to want to read."

Chris shut off the water and dried his hands on

the front of his pants. Kalina inwardly cringed at his lack of a dish towel but said nothing. She wasn't going to change things this late in the game.

"What's the article?" he asked.

"Why don't you just open it on your laptop? Easier to read that way."

He disappeared into the living room, returning a moment later with his laptop open and an internet browser waiting for the web address. She read it out to him and they both waited in silence as the page loaded. As soon as she saw the byline, Kalina let out an audible groan. She shouldn't have been surprised.

**Romance Kills Mood in Ellesworth**

By: Beth Finnegan, Staff Writer

Police are investigating a series of grisly murders that have rocked the town in the last few days. The bodies of two young women were found on the beach in the early morning hours, each dead from apparent head trauma. Each was missing their ring finger on their left hand. According to sources inside the department, both had recently become engaged.

In a grim twist, the victims' fingers were sent to members of the public, including newly sworn-in Captain Christian Harper. This isn't the first time a crime has hit close to home for the captain. Last summer, a series of murders led to the arrest and confession of former Captain Daniel Cahill, Harper's mentor. A source within the department who wishes to remain anonymous, confirmed that the victims' fiancés are persons of interest. Stay tuned for more updates as the investigation unfolds.

The color drained from Chris's face and his shoulder muscles tightened. Kalina couldn't blame him for the anger he was clearly feeling. She felt a sense of betrayal. Beth had done exactly what Kalina had told her not to do. And now it appeared there was a leak within the department. Just what Chris needed on his first official day as the head of the department.

"I can't believe she did this." His voice came out in a low growl.

"I told her she shouldn't write anything about this. Especially since she got one of the fingers," Kalina said. She wanted to ease his anger even though she knew it wasn't directed at her.

"This is why I hate reporters. Hell, whoever killed Gabriella and Margaret probably wanted this to happen. See his deeds in print."

"I suppose she was decent enough to keep their names out of it."

"For now. I don't doubt in whatever piece she runs next she'll be dragging them and their fiancés through the mud. And now our witness interviews could be compromised."

"I can try to talk to her if you want," Kalina offered.

"No. I'll handle it. I need to know who is giving her this information. None of it should be available to the public. I don't even think we have a confirmed autopsy on either victim yet."

"Take a breath, honey. She's just one reporter who wrote one story."

He ran his hands through his hair and linked his fingers behind his head. "She had to bring up Cahill. It has nothing to do with this investigation but she's calling my ability to be objective into question. It's like I'm too stupid to see what's right in front of me."

"You can't let her get in your head. This case is barely a day or two old and you are doing everything right. You'll find who talked to her and you'll deal with it. Now, why don't I go with you to the jewelry store? I actually bought some earrings for the wedding that I want them to insure."

"I need to get someone to track down Beth Finnegan. You don't know where she went do you?"

"No. When she left Geeks and Things she was heading out to get some air. I feel horrible that I didn't pay more attention to what she was doing."

"You aren't her babysitter, Kal. You were doing the department a favor even driving her somewhere.

This isn't on you. It's on us. And I swear we're going to make it right."

She stood up and planted a firm kiss on his lips. "You can make it right by catching whoever is doing this before they hurt anyone else."

## 10

Kalina let Chris drive her back to the shop with the agreement that he'd meet her there at four and they could go to the jeweler's together. It would give her time to wrap up business for the day and hopefully Chris would be able to figure out who'd given confidential information to Beth. Her gut told her it wasn't Jimmy. He looked up to Chris too much to spill the beans, even to a pretty reporter. It had to be someone else in the department but she couldn't put her finger on anyone specific. Everyone seemed as though they walked the straight and narrow. Just as she flipped the front door sign to "Open" her cell phone buzzed in her pocket. Her mother.

"Hi Mom."

"Did your sister tell you about the earrings?"

"Yes. I got them this morning. Chris and I are

going over later to make sure we get the paperwork for insurance purposes. Everything's going to be fine."

"I saw that article in the paper. How are you two holding up?"

Kalina let out a little sigh. "We're fine. Chris is just digging in to work. Not that I blame him."

"I just worry about you sometimes."

"And I know you'll never stop, no matter what I say. But I promise we're both safe. They're close to finding the person who did it." It was a lie but she knew it would assuage her mother's worry.

"As long as you're sure."

Kalina could see people approaching the front of the shop through the blinds on the front windows. "Mom, I've got to go. Customers await."

"OK. I love you."

Kalina ended the call and yanked the door open. Her nephew's rosy face greeted her. She quirked a brow at him but he said nothing, just stepped around her into the warmth of the shop. A few other people followed suit and, before she had closed the door, AJ jumped behind the counter and started taking orders. She settled in the corner and watched him dart around the shop like a pro. He kept a broad grin plastered to his face until the last customer had left the shop and the bell above the door quieted.

"You aren't supposed to be here," Kalina chided.

"I told Mom I left some stuff here yesterday."

"You shouldn't be lying to your mother."

"I know. But I saw that article on the news... Mom hasn't yet and I just wanted to see how you were holding up."

"I'm fine, kiddo. Chris is on the warpath but I don't blame him."

"It said there was a source in the police. Is that true?"

"I don't know. He's trying to find out."

On cue, her phone buzzed with a new text from Chris. "Leak in ME's office. Ex-boyfriend of reporter." "And it looks like they solved the leaky department problem."

"Why do you think she brought up Captain Cahill?"

"To try to draw attention to what's going on. It was a horrible thing for her to do. I should have realized she was going to write something even though I told her not to."

"It isn't your fault, Aunt K."

Tears welled in her eyes. "I just feel like I could have done more to keep her quiet."

AJ pulled her into a tight bear hug and she tightened her grip on him too. She wanted to tell him the truth about what was making her so emotional but she wanted to wait to share that news until everything was over, the wedding included.

"Do they have any leads?"

Kalina relinquished her grip on her nephew and

wiped at her eyes. "I'm not sure. From what I know, the fiancés are clear."

"So that reporter lied."

"Or she interpreted what she saw at the station when she was being interviewed."

"You and Chris will solve it. You always do."

She forced a watery smile. "Thanks for the vote of confidence." Kalina gave his arm an appreciative squeeze. "Now, you should get home before your mother has a heart attack because you aren't studying."

"Do I have to?"

"Yes. Move it, mister."

He pouted all the way to the front door but cracked a smile before wrapping his scarf over his mouth and heading out into the cold. As the door swung shut, she spotted Chris's car rolling up the block. He rolled down the passenger side window and leaned over. "You ready?"

"You're early."

"Didn't you see my text?"

"Yeah. But I thought you were going to try to talk to Beth again."

"I've got guys out looking for her. She's not with the ex-boyfriend and there's been no response at her house or office."

"Let me grab my coat."

The ride over to the jewelry store was short and quiet. Neither of them seemed to know what to say.

Kalina still couldn't shake the feeling that she should have done something more to stop Beth from posting the article. The anger that had made the lines of Chris's face sharper a few hours ago had dulled a little. At least no one under his direct command had blabbed to the press.

"I've got the fiancés coming back in to be questioned about their whereabouts on the days the other women went missing," Chris said as he pulled into a free spot in the parking lot. He chose the middle spot, equal distance from the door and the edge of the lot. She assumed it was to conceal his presence for as long as possible. There was only one other car in the lot.

"So how are we going to do this?" Kalina asked and unbuckled her seatbelt. She spotted a woman talking with Mr. Hempstead.

"I'll go in first and see what I can find out. You should just stay here."

She said nothing to his directive to stay in the car. They both knew it wasn't going to happen. But she waited while he climbed out of the car and headed for the only entrance to the small shop. With his back turned to her, Kalina ducked out of the car and inched up the sidewalk so she could try to catch snippets of the conversation.

"I told you, I'm done having this conversation," a woman's voice said.

"Is everything all right?" Chris's voice came through the partially opened front door.

"Fine. This is a private matter." Mr. Hempstead's tone was harsh.

"Are you sure you're OK, miss?"

No response but Kalina caught the woman's head bob up and down slightly.

"I was just going." The woman's voice filtered out into the open air. Kalina watched as Chris held the door open for her. She rushed out the front door and exhaled a long, clouded breath in the winter air. Kalina searched her coat pockets and found an unused tissue.

"Here." She offered it to the woman.

"Thanks."

Without a word, Kalina guided the woman out of view of the front door of the shop. The woman gave a hiccup and blew her nose loudly.

"I don't mean to pry but that didn't sound very good in there."

"Oh, that. It's nothing really. Just a little disagreement."

"Mr. Hempstead seemed pretty upset."

"He gets very passionate about things. Really, I'll be fine. Just if you wouldn't mind not telling him where I'm going. We both need some time to cool off."

"Sure thing." She fished for another tissue. "Just in case..."

"Fiona."

"Well then, just in case, Fiona."

After taking the proffered tissue, Fiona pulled out car keys, along with a hotel key card with a tree logo—which she promptly shoved back into her pocket—and the headlights flashed on the other car in the lot. Kalina waved her off before heading in to join Chris. She prayed he was having some luck questioning Mr. Hempstead.

The warmth of the shop greeted her as she walked in. Mr. Hempstead was nowhere to be seen but Chris waited at the counter, hands clasped in front of him.

"Hey. How's it going in here?"

"I'm taking a look at his books."

Kalina pointed to the display case of engagement rings, still with three empty spots. At least he hadn't sold any more since she'd last been in. "That's what I was talking about with the missing ring."

"I see." He glanced over his shoulder at the now empty parking lot. "Did you get anything out of the woman?"

"Her name is Fiona. I didn't get a last name. I think she and the owner are a couple. She seemed upset. But I think she's just going to cool off."

"I get kind of an odd vibe from this guy," Chris said in a whisper.

Mr. Hempstead appeared with the ledger in

hand and stopped short when he spotted Kalina. "You're back."

She smiled at him. "Yeah, I realized I wanted to ask you for information on insurance for the purchase I made the other day. But I see you're busy."

Mr. Hempstead waved his hand dismissively in Chris's direction. "It's fine. I'm sure the officer can wait."

"It's Captain, actually. And, no, I can't wait."

Kalina stepped back with her hands held up in a gesture of surrender. She was a little curious to see how Chris handled the jeweler with an audience again. And not someone he could push around. Color flooded the man's cheeks and he shoved the ledger across the counter to Chris. "Here's what you asked for. I still don't know what this has to do with that article in the paper."

Chris flipped through the pages and slid his finger down the item line on one page in particular. "I see you've got two individuals who purchased diamond engagement rings but I notice that there's a third one missing from the display."

"Is there a question in there somewhere?"

Chris set the ledger down and crossed his arms over his chest. "Did you sell a third ring to someone?"

"I don't remember."

Kalina caught the tightening of her fiancé's jaw

as he fought to control his temper. Mr. Hempstead was clearly trying to exert dominance in the conversation and it wasn't helping his case. After a tense moment, Chris said, "You keep meticulous records, Mr. Hempstead. I don't believe for one second you sold something and didn't record it. And you should know that, if you keep lying to me, I can have you arrested for obstructing a police investigation."

"I only record items once they are picked up, paid for and a one week period passes for returns. That hasn't happened for the third ring, yet."

"I'm still going to need the name of the person who placed the order."

"I don't have it on hand."

Before Chris could call him on his bluff, his phone rang. "Captain Harper."

Kalina could make out Jimmy's voice, albeit tinny and distorted over the open phone line. "Both of the guys came back in. They have alibis for the other dates. Should we cut them loose?"

"You're absolutely sure?" A pause and a garbled response that Kalina couldn't hear. Then, "OK. Fine. Any luck locating our missing witness?" Another pause and, by the crestfallen look that came over his face, the answer wasn't what he'd wanted. "Keep looking. I'll see you back at the station."

He ended the call and looked at Mr. Hempstead. "I'm going to come back and I expect you to have that information. If you don't, I'm going to arrest you. Do you understand?"

"Yes. Fine. Can I help my other customer now?"

"You know what... I'll just come back another time. There's really no rush. You clearly have more important things to deal with. Thanks again for the earrings," Kalina said and backed out of the shop as quickly as possible.

Chris followed once he was sure Mr. Hempstead wouldn't see them get into the car together. He walked outside and exhaled a slow breath. "He's hiding something. I know it."

"You think he knows who the third person is?"

"I do. And if the fiancés have been cleared, we're back to no suspects."

"This might sound crazy but could Mr. Hempstead have been involved?"

"I don't see how. Sure, he sold the rings but what motive would he have to kill them and cut off their fingers? He'd just made a lot of money on those rings. It's not like he could resell them," she said once they were back in the car on their way back to the station.

"There's just something in my gut telling me that something is off about this guy. And why has Beth Finnegan all of a sudden fallen off the face of the planet?"

"I will admit that's weird. Hey, do you think you could drop me off back at the shop?"

"Sure, but you should take it easy. I don't want you overexerting yourself."

She patted the hand that gripped the gear shift. "That's sweet of you but the baby and I are perfectly fine."

"And maybe I'm a little worried that whoever is going after people might go after you."

"They are recently engaged couples, Chris. We've been engaged for a while. We're getting married in two weeks. They aren't going to target me. Besides, even if they did, I know you'd hunt them down."

**11**

———

The shop was quiet, almost eerily so, when she walked back through the front door. The mystery of who had hurt the women was gnawing at her thoughts and wouldn't let go. There was a piece they were all missing but she was going to find it. She flipped the front door sign to "Closed" and settled in the game room with her tablet propped on her knees. She started with searching for Mr. Hempstead on Facebook. There couldn't be many guys with that name. Her search returned only three results and the first was the subject for her investigation. His profile picture showed him and Fiona—albeit younger than they both were now—cozied up on a couch. She clicked over to his profile page and saw that his most recent update was a relationship status change to "Engaged". He'd also posted a short engagement notice.

**Bruce Hempstead is pleased to announce his recent engagement to Fiona Hayes of Salem, Massachusetts. The couple has been together for ten years and are excited to forge their new path together as partners in marriage.**

At least Kalina had a last name for Fiona now. She saw that Fiona was tagged in the post and so she clicked the link. Curiously, Fiona hadn't updated her status or shown any indication that she was now engaged. Come to think of it, Kalina hadn't seen any engagement ring on Fiona's hand. Did this mean that Fiona's ring was the third one missing? If that were the case, then Mr. Hempstead was unlikely to have filed it in his ledger. It made sense but in the age of Internet over-sharing, it was strange that Fiona hadn't followed suit and told the world she was now spoken for. Kalina hit the back button to check the dates on Bruce's page. It was almost a month ago. Fiona's latest posts were from a couple days ago so there was definitely time to update if she'd wanted to.

"The engagement must have been what they were arguing about earlier," she said aloud.

So that was one mystery solved. At least to a point. That still left the larger one of the missing reporter. Leaving Facebook for now, Kalina searched for the town's online edition of the paper. Luckily, the list of staff writers and reporters was easily accessible at the top of the home page. She found Beth's name and a list of articles she'd authored filled the screen with "Read More" links after the introductory sentence. The article she'd written about Margaret and Gabriella's deaths was the top story. It also had the most views of any of her articles. She'd mostly written fluff pieces about town history and small events going on. She really did want to be a crime reporter.

Setting the tablet aside for the moment, Kalina retrieved her phone and placed a call to Chris's cell. He answered on the first ring.

"Everything OK?" He couldn't mask his worry.

"I'm fine but I found something that might be helpful."

"What did you find, Kal?"

"So it looks like, at least according to Bruce Hempstead's Facebook page, he and Fiona are engaged. He posted about the engagement and changed his status about a month ago."

"That would explain the missing third ring."

"But here's the thing. When I was talking to Fiona earlier, I didn't see a ring on her finger. And she hasn't updated her status or even acknowledged the engagement. Speaking from experience, that's not the kind of thing you really ignore or forget to mention."

"Maybe she just hasn't gotten to it yet."

"She's posted other stuff since he posted the engagement notice. I don't think she's going to post about it. Chris, what if he proposed and she said no?"

"It would certainly piss him off."

"And if he gave her a similar ring to the ones that Margaret and Gabriella received, seeing them happily flaunting them around town might push him over the edge."

"But to kill them? Why would he do that?"

"I don't know. But I think talking to him again isn't a bad idea."

"Yeah, I think you're right," he said.

"Did you have any luck finding Beth?"

"None. She's disappeared and I still can't figure out how."

"One thing at a time. Go find out why Mr. Hempstead is flaunting an engagement that sounds like it hasn't happened."

"Thanks for the heads up."

"Go save the day," she said and smiled.

She heard him chuckle on the other end of the line before it went dead and the call ended. Time to dig a little deeper into their missing wannabe crime reporter. One of the more recent articles was a piece on some of the more established families in town. Kalina opened the article and skimmed it, stopping near the end at a particularly interesting passage.

Perhaps the most influential families in town were the Finnegans and the Hempsteads. Both families were among the first to settle in town after it was established and have been interconnected for several generations. The most recent generation is by far the closest in the town's history. Despite a large age gap, the Finnegan and Hempstead cousins share Sunday dinner every week. Their bond is deeper than any other family in town. There is nothing each family wouldn't do for the other in their hour of need.

Kalina's throat went dry. Everything was starting to make sense. She'd have to double check town records but she was almost certain Beth and Bruce were related. Attacking Gabriella and Margaret would serve each of them in different ways. Maybe, in some twisted way, it would make Fiona say yes to Bruce's proposal and Beth would get her shot at becoming a crime reporter. The realization turned her stomach and bile burned the back of her throat. She forced it back down and grabbed her phone and keys. She had an idea of where Beth might be hiding and, if that were the case, Fiona was in more trouble than they realized. She tried Chris's cell again but it went to voicemail.

"Chris, I think I know what's going on and where to find Beth. Call me back."

## 12

Kalina's heart hammered against her rips as she yanked the driver side door open and tossed her phone onto the passenger seat. The car's engine fought her as she tried furiously to jam the keys into the ignition. "Come on!"

On the third try, the key slid into the slot and she was able to turn it, the engine rumbling to life. The tires squealed as she peeled out of the parking lot and turned onto Main Street. The tree symbol from the hotel key card danced in her vision. There was only one hotel in town. She didn't even need to look it up. The four-story building sat at the edge of town, leading toward the highway on and off ramps. It was a genius layout and the hotel's location also meant she saw it every time she came to town during college. She'd even stayed there a time or two when she stopped by and her parents were out of town.

Unfortunately, with all of the snow, the town maintenance hadn't gotten all of the roads cleared and her car swerved on unseen patches of black ice. Kalina's fingers gripped the steering wheel in a white-knuckled vice grip until the car righted itself and she slowed down. Beside her, the screen of her phone lit up with an incoming call. Chris's face flashed on the screen and she reached over and hit "Accept" and set the phone to speaker as she continued driving.

"Sorry I missed your call," her fiancé said over the phone line.

"Did you get to have your chat with Bruce Hempstead?"

"Nope. There was a sign on the front door saying he was going out of town for a few weeks and would be closed until then. He's in the wind."

"I know where Beth is hiding." The hotel's front entrance loomed ahead of her on the right hand side of the road. "The Elm Tree Lodge."

"How do you figure?"

"I did some digging into Beth and the type of articles she'd written. When we were going back to the shop she mentioned wanting to be a crime reporter. The rest of her work was mostly boring town fluff pieces. But she'd also done a history of the town's most influential families. The Hempsteads and the Finnegans were on the list. I think she and Bruce are cousins."

"This seems like a long shot, Kal."

"Just hear me out, OK? If we're right, and Bruce proposed to Fiona and she turned him down, then maybe seeing Gabriella and Margaret happily wearing the ring he'd chosen set him off. I think dear Cousin Beth offered to help him find a way to convince Fiona to change her mind and in exchange he'd give her something to launch her career as a crime reporter."

"You think all of her emotion at getting the severed finger was just a ruse?"

"I've seen better actresses"—her sister's ex college roommate Savannah came to mind—"but she's definitely believable. It's not hard to conjure tears over someone losing a finger."

"Let's say you're right. Where does the hotel come into play?"

"When I was talking to Fiona earlier, she pulled out her car keys and I saw a key card with the hotel's logo on it. I didn't think much of it then but that has to be where she's staying to keep away from Bruce. I can't imagine Beth would let her out of her sight for long."

"OK. I'm going to get some officers to check it out."

"I'm already here," Kalina said and nearly strangled herself in her effort to get out of the car. "I'll see what I can find."

"Kalina, do not go in there. This situation just got

a lot more dangerous." His tone took on a more emotional tone. "You aren't just thinking about yourself anymore. You have our child to consider. Please let me take it from here on out."

"OK." She wouldn't be interfering by just sitting in the lobby. If she was lucky she could find out what room Fiona was in. And Beth certainly couldn't be in the room with her, could she?

"I mean it, Kal. Stay out of it."

"I will."

She ended the call and stowed her phone in her coat pocket before heading through the revolving doors into the warm air of the lobby. It was just as she remembered with the warm, muted browns and reds in the carpet and furniture. Even the wood of the front desk had been stained a deep cherry color. A tired looking man stood in the reception area. Beth was nowhere in sight. That worried her a little. Kalina sidled up to the reception desk and leaned forward, chin propped in one hand.

"Checking in?" the desk clerk asked.

"No, I was actually looking for a friend of mine. Fiona Hayes. She mentioned she was staying here for a few days. She said I could stop by if I had time."

"I'm not supposed to give out guest information."

"Oh, I know. Guest privacy is very important. But she told me what the number was but I can't remember." She pulled out her phone and made a show of searching through her notes app. "I swear I put it in here but I think it got deleted. I had to do a restore on this stupid thing the other day. Such a pain."

The clerk gave a long sigh but turned to the computer and hit a few keys. "She's in room 117. Down the hall to the left."

"That's right. Thanks so much!" She kept her phone out and headed down the hallway he'd indicated.

The hall was pretty quiet except for the occasion blare of a TV. She reached a junction where rooms 113-121 branched. She approached slowly, staying to the far side of the hall, when a loud crash echoed ahead. She had a sinking feeling it had come from room 117.

## 13

Kalina paused across the hall from room 117. Nothing came after the crash and she suddenly realized that she had no way of getting into the room. She had no key and if either Beth or Bruce was inside with Fiona, they wouldn't be letting her in willingly. Chewing her bottom lip, she glanced back down the hallway and back to the door. The silence was broken by a woman's scream coming from the room in front of her.

"That's it."

She barreled back down the hallway to the lobby. The clerk stared at her with only a mild interest. "I just heard a scream coming from Fiona's room."

"Probably the TV."

"No. I don't think so. Do you have a master key or something?"

"Look lady, I'm starting to think you don't even know her."

"OK, you're right. I don't really know her that well. But I know she's in trouble. Her boyfriend has been violent before and she's been staying here because they've been fighting. I think he's found her." She searched her phone for anything with a picture of Bruce. She finally settled on the "About Us" page from the jewelry store website. "This is what he looks like."

The clerk took the phone and studied the picture. The color that had been in his cheeks a moment before drained in an instant. "He came here about a half hour ago. But he wasn't meeting the woman in 117. He was here to see some reporter. She rented out 119."

"Do they connect?"

"Yes, but they're locked."

"How hard is it to jimmy them open?"

"If you know what you're doing, probably not hard."

Kalina let out a groan at the revelation that, as long as Beth knew which room Fiona was in, all she'd need to do was get the adjoining room. "Get a key for 119 then. And whatever you need to unlock the door between the two rooms."

"Shouldn't we like call the police or something?"

"They're already on their way. Now come on. A woman's life depends on you moving your ass."

The clerk fumbled for a set of key cards and a regular metal key and followed after her down the hallway. The hall was silent again and that unnerved her. Kalina motioned for him to unlock 119. He dropped the key card three times before she yanked it from his fingers and slid it into the lock. The little light turned green and she eased it open as quietly as she could. It turned out they didn't need the metal key for the doors separating the rooms; the one leading from room 119 was already open. Kalina waved the clerk back. "Wait for the police," she whispered.

He backpedaled out of the room and she heard muffled footsteps going back down the hallway. She held her breath and pressed her ear to the door leading into room 117. She could hear shallow breathing and then a loud whimper.

"I did what you wanted." Bruce's voice was low and strained.

"Not enough." Beth's tone was far more authoritative than Kalina had heard her before.

"Says you. You have more than enough to take you as far as you want."

"We shouldn't be discussing this in here. In front of her."

"She won't say anything. Will you, sweetheart?"

A muffled whimper answered him. Did they have Fiona tied up and gagged? The image in her head was almost enough to give her away. Footsteps thudded toward the dividing door and Kalina pressed herself to the wall so that when the door swung inward it would hide her. She bit her tongue to keep from breathing too loudly as the door swung in and Beth pushed past. She didn't seem to notice Kalina and neither did Bruce as he trudged after her, something shiny gripped in his hand. The door on the room 119 side closed and Kalina exhaled slowly. As quietly as she could, she slipped around the door and into the next room. Fiona sat on the bed, her left hand cradled to her chest. Her eyes shone with tears and her cheeks were pale. It became readily apparent what had happened as soon as Kalina held a finger to her lips for quiet and Fiona meekly raised her left arm a little. A hotel towel was wrapped around her hand.

"Let me see," Kalina whispered.

"He … they are insane," Fiona moaned.

"Shh. I'm going to get you out of here but I need to see what happened." As gently as possible, she unwrapped the towel and had to swallow back a new batch of bile. Fiona's ring finger was missing just above the second knuckle. Just like Gabriella and Margaret.

"The police are on their way. As soon as we're out of here, I'm going to call for an ambulance."

"He still has it."

Kalina's brow wrinkled in confusion. Then it hit her. The shiny item clutched in Bruce's hand had been her severed finger and the engagement ring. She prayed that Chris would arrive soon and apprehend Bruce before he did something even crazier.

Kalina helped Fiona scoot off the bed and wrapped the towel around her hand again to stem the bleeding. Together they eased their way out the front door of the hotel room and started toward the lobby. Fiona was uneasy on her feet due to the blood loss, which slowed them down. They were almost at the junction when a door slammed open behind them and Bruce appeared wielding a knife in one hand and Fiona's finger in the other. Without thinking, Kalina put herself in front of the injured woman.

His knife hand faltered an inch. "You?"

"It's over, Mr. Hempstead. The police are already on their way. You and Beth aren't going to get away with what you've done."

"And I thought I was the only one who had the chops to be an investigative reporter," Beth said from behind Bruce. She stepped up beside her cousin and brandished a gun.

Heavy footsteps thudded behind Kalina and she didn't have to turn to know that the police had arrived just in time to back her play.

"Put your weapons down and get on the floor," Jimmy ordered. His service weapon was held high, aimed right at Bruce's chest.

Bruce's lower lip trembled and he tossed the

knife aside. As he got to his knees, he pressed Fiona's finger to his chest. "I love you."

Beth remained standing, weapon still pointing at the cluster of police. Jimmy's aim moved to her and after a moment she relented and tossed the weapon aside. Two uniformed officers approached and cuffed them.

Ambulance sirens wailed in the distance and Kalina turned to look at Jimmy. "Thank you." She flung her arms around his shoulders and held him close.

**14**

———

efore long, paramedics huddled around Fiona, one of them packing her finger in ice for transport. Despite the amount of blood, they seemed confident it could be reattached without much issue. That was small consolation considering what the man who claimed to love her had put her through. Kalina wasn't certain but had an inkling that Beth had been the one to push him to such extremes. Of the two, she had the more dominant personality. Both of them had already been led away in handcuffs by the time Kalina trailed Fiona and the paramedics out to the parking lot. Just as the ambulance peeled away, lights flashing and sirens wailing anew, Chris's car came screaming into the lot. He pulled to a stop across several parking spaces and her cheeks burned with color.

"Please tell me you are OK," he said and grabbed her by the wrists.

"I'm fine."

He frantically checked her over for signs of injury. His hand stopped on a few splatters of blood on her jacket. She hadn't even noticed it there.

"Chris, it's not mine, I swear. Bruce Hempstead cut off Fiona's finger. She had her hand wrapped in a towel. It must have gotten on me when I took a look."

"I told you to stay put and let the police handle this, Kal."

"If I hadn't then maybe they would have done worse than they did." She didn't mean to start yelling at him.

Chris tightened his grip on her wrist and pulled out of view of the other officers still on scene. As soon as they were alone, he let go. "I know you like to help and I can't say that it hasn't been invaluable but this was really dangerous. They could have gone after you."

"But they didn't. They didn't even know I was there until the end. And by then Jimmy had already showed up. I helped that woman survive a trauma and I'm not going to apologize for it. Be angry at me if you have to. That's fine. But I'm not going to say I'm sorry when it would be a lie."

Chris exhaled a long, slow breath and scrubbed at his face with the heels of his hands. "The more you get involved the more I worry something is going to happen. And with the baby now... I can't do my job if I'm constantly worrying about you. Do you understand that?"

"I do. Of course I understand, Chris. And I never meant to make you worry or put me ahead of the needs of the job. Look, I'm going to go back to the shop and let you finish up here. We can talk about it when we get home."

She didn't give him time to respond before she dug the car keys out of her coat pocket and headed for her car. The streets were empty as she made the short journey back to Geeks and Things. The shop felt almost lonely as she settled in behind the counter to do a cash count. She didn't regret taking action to save Fiona. There was no way she could have sat by and let them hurt her further. She tried to understand what would motivate someone to start cutting off body parts of the people they loved but let the train of thought derail quickly. It was too disturbing to consider. She also couldn't believe Beth was willing to throw away a career as a journalist just to get ahead in the business.

**15**

———————

The house had been tense for a few days after Fiona's rescue but Kalina and Chris managed to reconcile. They were both just relieved that they weren't receiving severed fingers in the mail any longer. It also didn't hurt that Fiona was going to make a full recovery with a little physical therapy. At present, Kalina stood off to the side as AJ manned the register. His imposed time away was now over and she was even happier to have him back for many reasons, not least of which was because she was under strict orders not to touch anything. Jillian had meticulously done Kalina's hair and nails for the wedding that afternoon and her sister would kill her if she messed them up.

"I think that's the last one," AJ said as he shut the cash register and leaned on his elbows.

Before Kalina could express her relief at the

empty shop, the front door opened again and Fiona walked in. Her hand was bandaged but she looked better. A few days in the hospital had actually done her good.

"I can handle this, kiddo. Go get ready for this afternoon," Kalina said and stepped behind the register.

AJ darted past her and out through the back of the shop. Kalina tried not to fuss with her hair and nails and Fiona rested her injured hand on the counter.

"I just wanted to come by and thank you properly," Fiona said.

"You don't have to do that. I'm just glad everything is going to be OK."

"I should have known something was off when Bruce kept pushing for me to accept his proposal."

"Not that it's any of my business but can I ask why you didn't?"

"Marriage isn't something I wanted. It's just not part of my life plan. I thought he understood that."

"I'm sorry this happened to you."

"I'm just sorry you had to get dragged into it."

Kalina bit her tongue to keep from retorting that she'd jumped in with both feet. Over Fiona's right shoulder, Kalina spotted a taxi cab. "So are you heading out of town?"

"Yeah. I'm going to stay with my parents for a while. I'm thinking of moving out of state too. I know

Massachusetts is a big place but right now it feels like everywhere I turn he's there. I need a fresh start. I suppose it's small comfort that Bruce is taking a deal. He'll do some time and I don't have to testify."

"Well, I hope things work out for you."

Fiona dabbed at the corners of her eyes to ward off tears. "Thanks. I should let you go. It looks like you have somewhere to be."

"I'm actually getting married today." She couldn't hide the wide smile or her nerves.

"You're going to make a beautiful bride."

Kalina stepped out from behind the counter and gave Fiona a firm parting hug. They walked out to Main Street and Kalina waved Fiona off as she climbed into the back of the cab and headed in the direction of the highway. Blowing out a breath to settle her nerves, Kalina made the trek to her parents' house.

In her effort to keep her hair and nails intact, she'd worked up a bit of a sweat on the way over. Her mother fussed over her as she changed into her dress. It was a simple dress with cap sleeves and a modest neckline. She hadn't wanted to spend much on the dress even though her mother insisted she should get whatever dress she wanted. She fastened the emerald earrings into place and studied her reflection. Bruce Hempstead may have been delusional but he did have an eye for beautiful jewelry. She had to give him that.

"You look so beautiful," her mother said, wiping tears off her cheeks.

"Thanks."

"I can't believe this day is finally here. I didn't think it would come, Kal," Jillian said with a wry smile.

Kalina just rolled her eyes and laughed. Time to tie the knot and start her future with the man she loved. The church was only partly filled; they hadn't invited too many people. As the organist began the processional, everyone stood and turned their attention to her. She let out a breath and gripped her mother's arm. The only thing that could have made the day even better was if her father had been there to walk her down the aisle. But he was with them in spirit. Chris stood at the front of the church, Jimmy by his side. She couldn't help but beam up at both of them as she and her mother started down the aisle.

She studied the faces as she passed. Most were friends from college and business school and some of the other officers in town who had come up through the academy with Chris. Nadine stood near the very front row, smiling a big, toothy grin as Kalina passed. Letting go of her mother's arm, she leaned over and pulled her friend into a tight embrace. She was grateful that Nadine was back in her life, even if it had taken tragedy to reunite them.

Chris drummed his fingers against his wrist until Kalina let go and finished her procession up to the front of the church. As discreetly as possible, Kalina wiped the sweat from her palms on the front of her dress before taking Chris's hands in hers.

The officiant cleared his throat and began. "We are gathered here today to witness the union of Kalina and Christian. Is there anyone assembled here today who can show just cause why these two should not be joined in marriage?"

The church was silent. Kalina squeezed Chris's hands and he returned the gesture. The officiant nodded after another few seconds had passed. "Then Kalina and Christian have chosen to share brief vows with each other and exchange rings as a symbol of their devotion to each other."

Kalina turned to take the wedding band from Jillian and placed it on Chris' finger. "Christian Harper, I take you as my husband, with your faults and your strengths, as I offer myself to you with my faults and my strengths. I will help you when you need help, and turn to you when I need help. For richer or poorer, in sickness and in health, I choose you as the person with whom I will spend my life."

Chris took her wedding band from Jimmy and slid it onto her left ring finger. They both stared at it for a brief moment before he, too, recited his vows. "Kalina Greystone, I take you as my wife, with your faults and your strengths, as I offer myself to you with my faults and my strengths. I will help you when you need help, and turn to you when I need help. For richer or poorer, in sickness and in health, I choose you as the person with whom I will spend my life."

"Having shared these vows and exchanged rings, by the power vested in me by the Commonwealth of Massachusetts, and in the sight of those assembled, I pronounce you husband and wife. You may kiss the bride."

Chris pulled her tight to him and planted a kiss on her lips. It seemed to last forever, just the two of them, and then the recessional music blared from the organ at the back of the church and they paraded down the aisle, arm-in-arm, ready to begin their lives as a married couple and take on the next chapter of their lives. In no time at all they were going to be parents and Kalina couldn't wait to see what that new journey brought.

**A graveyard discovery rocks Kalina's reality as she grapples with the past she thought she knew. Can she solve one last case and give a driving family closure?**

Download Saints and Sinners and try to save the day one last time today.

# GET FREE CONTENT

Sign up for my newsletter by clicking here to be kept up-to-date with my latest releases and receive your copy of Toil and Trouble as a free gift.

All Hallow's Eve brings dangerous secrets. Can Kalina get to the bottom of the mystery?

Subscribe and find out now!

# ABOUT THE AUTHOR

S.E. Biglow is the pen name of *USA Today* bestselling author Sarah Biglow. She lives in Massachusetts with her husband and son. She is a licensed attorney and spends her days combatting employment discrimination as an Investigator with the Massachusetts Commission Against Discrimination.

You can find an up-to-date list of all my books here